Play time

Catherine and Laurence Anholt

Would you like to play with me?

Share the biscuits, picnic tea?

Look down at the world below.

Hurry up now, don't be slow.

Yellow paint, and red and green.

You'll be king and I'll be queen.

Take our teddies for a ride.

Can you find me if I hide?

Banging, crashing, what a noise!

Watching quietly with my toys.

We are building in the snow.

I can cycle, watch me go!

Hop and skip and leap and jump.

Climb and hold and slide and bump.

We are dancing, come and look.